HOW
LITTLE GREY RABBIT
GOT BACK HER TAIL

By Alison Uttley
Pictures by Margaret Tempest

templar publishing

ONE COLD MARCH MORNING, Little Grey Rabbit awoke at dawn, for this was to be a busy day.

Softly she opened her door and listened. Snores could be heard coming from Hare's room, and squeaky little grunts from Squirrel's.

She crept downstairs, took down a round wicker basket and went out into the raw air.

The sun had not yet risen, and a single star still shone in the sky, "like a candle for a little rabbit," she thought.

As she walked down the garden path she looked back at the shut windows and waved a paw to her sleeping friends in the little house.

She turned down the lane and scampered over the stones, leaping over thorny briars and swinging her basket round and round above her head.

A startled mouse gazed after her. "I wonder where she is going? It's a pity she's lost her tail. They say it is fastened on Wise Owl's door as a knocker."

Grey Rabbit came to an opening in a hedge and climbed through, tearing her apron on a thorn. She stopped to pin it with a pin from a hawthorn bush, and to sip some water from a gurgling spring, like a small fountain in the grass.

Then she ran across the meadow to a bank where the first primroses were growing. She began to pick them, biting off their pink stalks, and filling her basket with yellow blossoms.

Suddenly a black nose and two pink hands poked up in front of her.

"Oh! Oh! Moldy Warp, how you frightened me!" she exclaimed, with her paw on her fluttering heart.

"What are you doing out here so early, Grey Rabbit?" asked the mole.

"I am picking primroses for primrose wine. Hare has a bad cold and it is a certain cure."

"What a clever rabbit you are!" said Moldy Warp admiringly. "But where is your tail?"

"I gave it to Wise Owl," she replied. "He told me where to get carrot seed."

"Oh! He did, did he?" muttered the mole. "Grey Rabbit, would you like your tail back very much?"

"Very, very much," answered Grey Rabbit sadly.

"I'll help you," said the mole, just as a long sunray shone across the field and turned his velvet waistcoat red. "I will think out a plan."

"Thank you, Moldy Warp. I must run now, or I shall be late for breakfast." And off she went with her flowers bobbing up and down in the basket.

In the little house by the wood, Squirrel and Hare couldn't find Little Grey Rabbit anywhere.

Hare ran up and down stairs with his head in a red cotton handkerchief, calling, "Where are you, Grey Rabbit? A-tishoo! Are you hiding? A-tishoo!"

But Squirrel saw Grey Rabbit's basket was gone, and guessed she must be busy somewhere.

"Help me to get the breakfast, Hare," she scolded.

13

Hare wiped his eyes and sneezed violently. "A-tishoo!" he went, then he swept the tablecloth off the table and wrapped it round his shoulders.

"Oh, do be careful!" exclaimed Squirrel, seizing the cloth and shaking it.

Just then, there was a *rat-a-tat-tat* at the door. It was Hedgehog with the milk.

"Late again!" said Squirrel. "Have you seen Grey Rabbit?"

Hedgehog shook his old head. "No," said he, "is she missing?"

"Of course she is, or I should not ask you," snapped Squirrel.

"Sorry, no offence," said Hedgehog, picking up his milk cans. "I can't abide that pair," he muttered as he set off. "Now, Grey Rabbit is a nice little thing."

He heard light footsteps coming up the lane, and a voice singing:

> "Primroses, primroses,
> Primroses fine,
> Pick them and press them
> And make yellow wine."

"Good morning, Hedgehog!" said Grey Rabbit, as she ran to the house. "Hare! Squirrel! Look at my primroses, picked with dew on them. Now we can make primrose wine to cure your cold, Hare!"

All day long they made the wine. Grey Rabbit packed the primroses in a wooden cask. Between each layer she put an acorn-cup of honey and a squeeze of wood-sorrel juice.

Squirrel filled the kettle from the brook and put it on the fire. Grey Rabbit poured boiling water over the flowers until the cask was full. Then she sealed it with beeswax and buried it in the garden.

"When can we have some?" asked Hare, as they sat down to tea.

"In twenty-four hours," said Little Grey Rabbit, and Hare began counting the minutes.

That night, Wise Owl flew over the house.

"Too-whit, a-tishoo!" he cried. "Too-whoo, a-tishoo!"

"Poor Wise Owl," murmured Grey Rabbit, tucked in her blanket. "He has a cold too. I must take him a bottle of primrose wine."

The next day, Squirrel worked in the garden, sowing fresh dandelion and lettuce seeds.

Hare sat sneezing by the fire, playing noughts and crosses against himself. He always won, so he was happy.

Little Grey Rabbit sat in her rocking chair mending her torn apron.

At last Squirrel came in, stamping her feet.

"It's bitter today, Grey Rabbit. And look at my tail! Where's my teasel brush? It's time you got me another."

After dinner, Grey Rabbit left Hare explaining noughts and crosses to Squirrel, who could never understand.

Away she went, through the wood with her basket. She stopped to look longingly at a horse-chestnut tree whose sticky buds were beyond her reach.

Then she ran through the gate and into the teasel field, where she bit off some prickly teasel heads and put them in her basket.

Home she ran, stepping on the soft moss.

"Robin Redbreast has been with a letter for you," said Squirrel.

Grey Rabbit took the leaf-envelope and broke open the brown flap.

"It's Moldy Warp's writing," she said. "It reads 'Found Knock Mole'."

"Whatever can it mean?" they all asked.

Hare said, "Moldy Warp has been found knocked over."

Squirrel said, "Mr Knock has found a mole."

Grey Rabbit said, "Mole has found a knock, but who has lost one?"

As evening wore on, Hare got more and more excited, until he could hardly bear to wait to dig up the cask of primrose wine.

When the seals were at last broken, such a delicious smell came into the room, like pine forests and honeysuckle and lime trees in flower. They filled their glasses with the golden wine.

"Good, good," said Hare. "I feel better already."

Then Little Grey Rabbit filled a bottle and tucked it under her arm to take to Wise Owl.

It was dark and the wood was full of rustles and murmurs. Grey Rabbit felt very frightened, for they were not comfortable, homely sounds.

"A-tishoo! A-tishoo!" came echoing through the trees, and Grey Rabbit caught sight of Owl. And her own little white tail was hanging on his front door.

"I've brought you some primrose wine for your sneeze," she said.

"Thank you kindly, Grey Rabbit. What would you like in return?"

Little Grey Rabbit hesitated and looked at her tail.

"No, I could not part with that. Not unless you bring me a bell to go *ting-a-ling-ling* when visitors call. But here is a book of riddles for you."

Grey Rabbit ran home with the book in her paw, but her thoughts full of the bell.

Squirrel and Hare were waiting for her, and between them, sipping from a teacup, sat Moldy Warp.

"Here she comes! Mole has something for you," exclaimed Hare.

Mole brought out a large silver penny. "It's Roman," he said. "I thought it would do for Wise Owl's door knocker."

"Oh, Moldy Warp, how kind. But Wise Owl will only give me back my tail in exchange for a bell."

"A bell? Where can we get a bell?" wondered Moldy Warp.

"There's a bell in the village shop," remembered Grey Rabbit.

"There are harebells, bluebells and Canterbury bells in the fields," said Hare.

"I might make a bell," said the mole, holding the penny in his strong hands. "I will bend it and twist it with my fingers till—"

And he walked musingly out of the house.

"Good night!" everyone called after him, but he only said, "And bend it and twist it," as he went slowly down the garden path.

Hare took the book of riddles to bed with him, and prepared to astonish Squirrel with a joke.

But when he awoke without his *a-tishoo*, he felt so grateful to Grey Rabbit that he got up early and went out into the fields to look for bells.

After breakfast, Squirrel announced, "I'm going to the village shop to get that bell."

"Oh, Squirrel!" exclaimed Grey Rabbit. "Please don't. The old woman might catch you."

But Squirrel put on her best yellow dress and her little blue shoes, and tied her tail with a bow of blue ribbon. Then she ran with a hop and a skip down the lane until she reached the village.

Presently a woman came out of a cottage and pushed open the shop door. *Tinkle, tinkle* went the bell, as Squirrel darted inside.

She leaped up and landed on the bell, which jangled loudly as it swung to and fro. She kicked her shoes off and lost her blue bow as she bit and tugged and pushed. At last the bell, with Squirrel still hanging onto it, fell to the floor, knocking over three buckets and a basket of eggs.

The shopkeeper shrieked. "That creature has got my bell!" she cried.

Squirrel picked up the noisy bell and ran out of the door, jingle-jangling through the market-place. She banged and bumped along the road, up the lane, through the garden and into the house.

Squirrel was a heroine that day.

But when Hare and Grey Rabbit dragged the bell across the wood to Wise Owl's door, he put his head out with half-shut eyes and hooted, "Who's making all that hullabaloo? How can I sleep with that jingle-jangle? Take it away!" And he slammed his door so that the little white tail shook.

When the dejected Hare and Grey Rabbit got home they found Moldy Warp talking to Squirrel.

He had brought a little silver bell made from the old coin. It had a tiny clapper of a hawthorn stone hung on a hair from a white mare's tail. When Moldy Warp shook the bell, a sweet silvery tinkle came from it.

Grey Rabbit started off to see Wise Owl as soon as it was dusk. She felt no fear as she carried the bell through the wood, for the wood held its breath to listen.

"What is that?" asked Wise Owl, as he peered down from his branch.

"A bell for my tail," said Grey Rabbit boldly, and she tinkled the little silver bell.

Owl climbed down. "You shall have your tail, Grey Rabbit. Give me the bell. It is beautiful, and it is wise, for it lived in the beginning of the world."

He hung the bell on his front door, and gave Grey Rabbit her tail in exchange, fastening it on with threads of stitchwort. By the time Little Grey Rabbit reached home again her tail was as good as ever.

Moldy Warp smiled, and took with him to his house under the green fields a bottle of primrose wine and the thanks of them all.

A TEMPLAR BOOK

This edition first published in the UK in 2012 by Templar Publishing,
an imprint of The Templar Company Limited,
The Granary, North Street, Dorking, Surrey, RH4 1DN, UK
www.templarco.co.uk

Original edition first published in the UK in 1930 by William Heinemann

This edition edited by *Susan Dickinson* and *Emily Hawkins*
Additional design by *janie louise hunt*

1 3 5 7 9 10 8 6 4 2

ISBN 978-1-84877-261-8

Printed in China